This book
belongs to

....

....

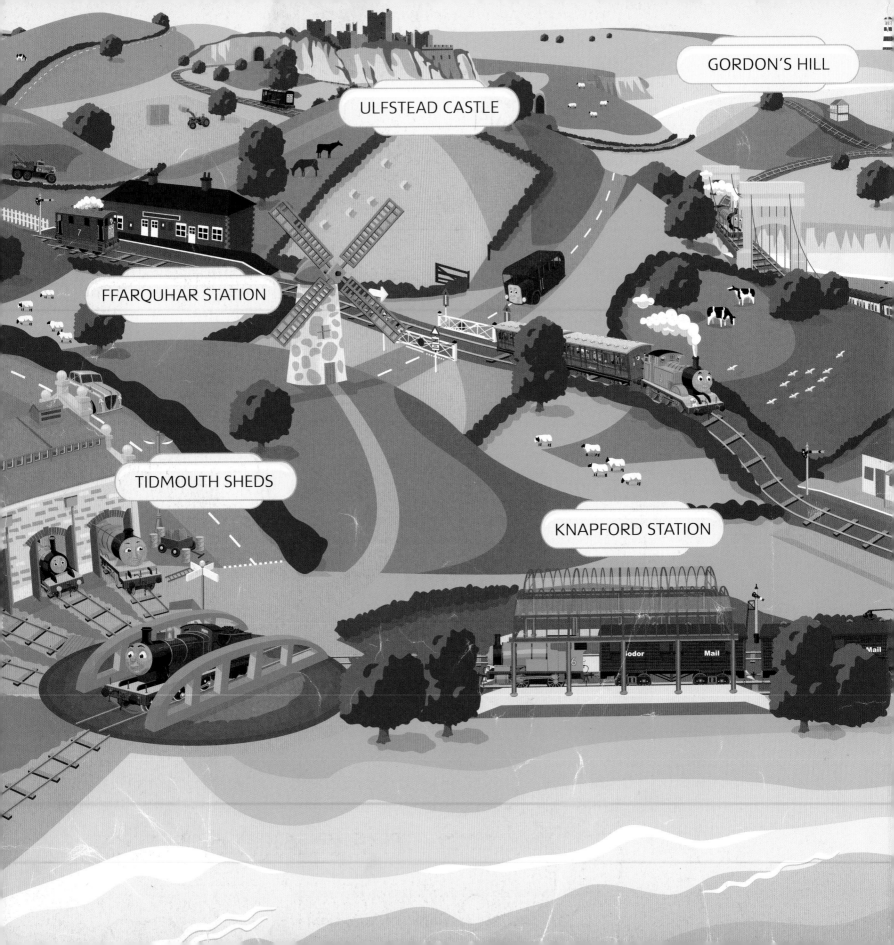

GORDON'S HILL

ULFSTEAD CASTLE

FFARQUHAR STATION

TIDMOUTH SHEDS

KNAPFORD STATION

CHINA CLAY PITS

BRENDAM DOCKS

DRYAW STATION

THE ISLAND OF SODOR

EGMONT
We bring stories to life

First published in 2019 in Great Britain by Egmont
The Yellow Building, 1 Nicholas Road, London W11 4AN

Written by Helen Archer
Designed by Martin Aggett
Illustrated by Robin Davies
Map illustration by Dan Crisp

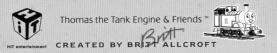

Thomas the Tank Engine & Friends ™

HiT entertainment   CREATED BY BRITT ALLCROFT

Based on the Railway Series by the Reverend W Awdry
© 2019 Gullane (Thomas) LLC.
Thomas the Tank Engine & Friends and Thomas & Friends
are trademarks of Gullane (Thomas) Limited.
© 2019 HIT Entertainment Limited. HIT and the HIT logo are
Trademarks of HIT Entertainment Limited.
All rights reserved.

ISBN 978 1 4052 9333 4

70342/001

Printed in Poland

THOMAS THE TANK ENGINE
Happy Birthday

This is a story about Thomas, the cheeky blue engine, and the day his friends threw him a very special party ...

It had been a very busy day on Sodor when Thomas puffed into the station at Maron.

"I'm sorry Thomas, but you're not finished yet," said The Fat Controller. "I need you to pick up Annie and Clarabel and get some trucks to the Quarry."

"I'll be as quick as I can," called Thomas as he pulled away.

Thomas worked really hard! He pulled Annie and Clarabel from one side of the Island to the other ...

shunted trucks to the Quarry ...

… and **coupled up** with Annie and Clarabel again to take them home.

When Thomas returned to the Sheds, he was too tired to talk to his friends and went straight to sleep.

The other trains were worried.

"Thomas has been working so hard," said James, "and it's his birthday soon."

"We should do something nice for him," chimed Gordon.

"I've got an idea!" exclaimed Percy.

The next day, everyone gathered in the yard to talk about the big plan.

"I can't wait to see Thomas' face!" tooted Bertie.

"Don't forget that it's a surprise, Bertie," warned Emily, "You mustn't tell Thomas."

"I won't," said Bertie. He couldn't wait for his part in Thomas' big surprise but he was worried he might give the secret away.

Later that day, Thomas was just about to
pull away from Knapford Station when he
noticed Bertie arriving.

"Hello Bertie,"
called Thomas.

"Oh ... can't stop!" said Bertie, sheepishly and he shot off down the road.

"Bertie must want me to race him!" exclaimed Thomas as he sped away after him.

Bertie was **worried** that he would give away the surprise so he drove away as fast as he could.

But Thomas' wheels were turning *faster* and *faster* and *faster*.

Thomas was close to **catching up** when ...

Bertie turned off the road beside the track and **zoomed off** away from Thomas.

Thomas didn't know what to do. Normally Bertie loved to race with him.

"Maybe Bertie doesn't want to be friends with me anymore."

That night, Thomas puffed **very slowly** and **very sadly** back to the Sheds.

In the morning, The Fat Controller asked Thomas to come all the way to the Steamworks to meet him.

"**Go faster, we're late!**"
grumbled Annie and Clarabel.

"**Must hurry. Must hurry!**"
puffed Thomas. He was feeling very
tired after his busy week.

"There you are Thomas," said The Fat Controller when Thomas arrived at the Steamworks, **"we need to smarten you up."**

... and so his dome was **polished ...**

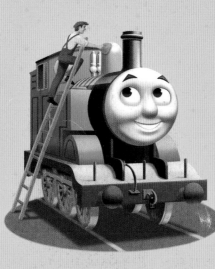

... he was given a smart **new coat of paint ...**

... his buffers were **buffed ...**

... and he was given **brand new, shiny wheels!**

"Now you're ready," said The Fat Contoller.

"Ready for what?" asked Thomas.

"Happy birthday Thomas," cheered The Fat Controller as they pulled up to the party.

"Surprise!" shouted Bertie from the platform.

"I'm **sorry** I didn't race with you the other day Thomas, but I didn't want you to know about your surprise birthday party."

It was a **wonderful party!** All of Thomas' friends wished him a very happy birthday and even sang to him.

"Happy birthday to you.
Happy birthday to you ..."

"That was a good party,"
said James that night.

"Did you have fun, Thomas?" asked Bertie.

But Thomas didn't reply. He had already fallen asleep, thinking how lucky he was to have such good friends.

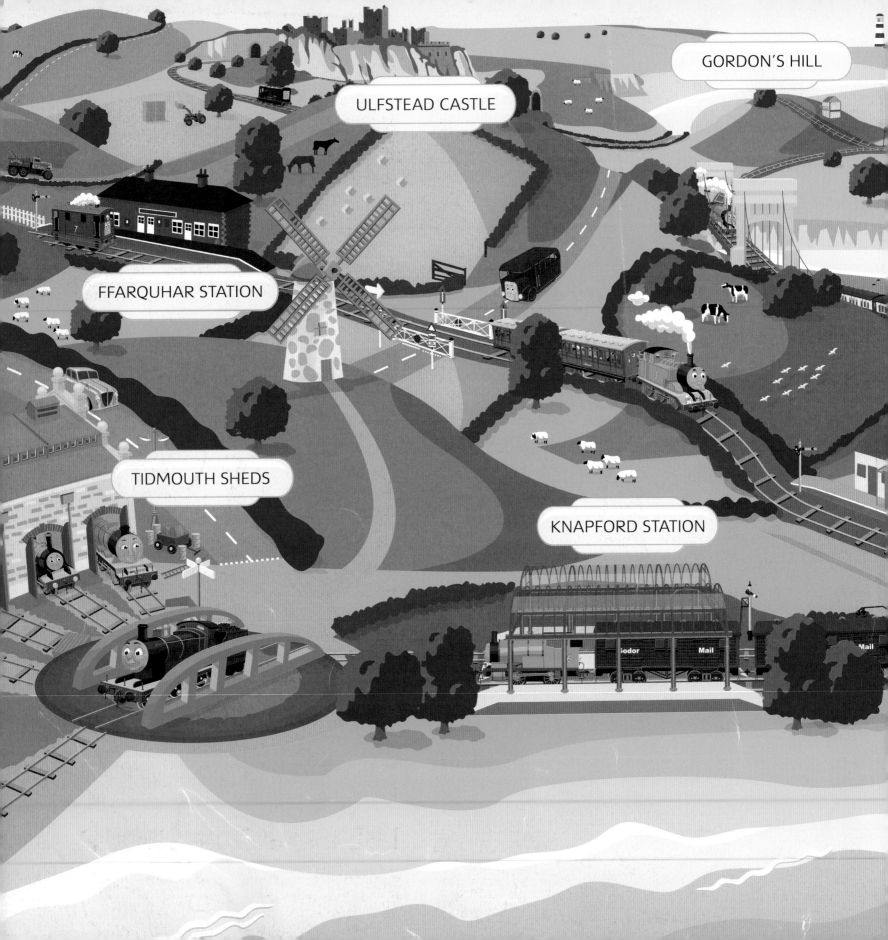

GORDON'S HILL

ULFSTEAD CASTLE

FFARQUHAR STATION

TIDMOUTH SHEDS

KNAPFORD STATION

CHINA CLAY PITS

BRENDAM DOCKS

DRYAW STATION

THE ISLAND OF SODOR

About the author

The Reverend W. Awdry was the creator of 26 little books about Thomas and his famous engine friends, the first being published in 1945. The stories came about when the Reverend's two-year-old son Christopher was ill in bed with the measles. Awdry invented stories to amuse him, which Christopher then asked to hear time and time again. And now for 70 years, children all around the world have been asking to hear these stories about Thomas, Edward, Gordon, James and the many other Really Useful Engines.

The Three Railway Engines, first published in 1945.

The Reverend Awdry with some of his readers at a model railway exhibition.